The Boy
& His Mud Horses

& Other Stories from the Tipi

Told and Illustrated by Paul Goble

Foreword by Albert White Hat, Sr.

World Wisdom

Most recent printing indicated by the last digit below:
10 9 8 7 6 5 4 3 2

for Arial Marie

Library of Congress Cataloging-in-Publication Data

Goble, Paul.
  The boy & his mud horses : & other stories from the tipi / told and
illustrated by Paul Goble ; foreword by Albert White Hat Sr.
    p. cm.
  Includes bibliographical references.
  ISBN 978-1-935493-11-2 (hardcover : alk. paper) 1. Indians of North
America--Great Plains--Folklore--Juvenile literature. 2. Folklore--Great
Plains--Juvenile literature. I. Title. II. Title: Boy and his mud horses.
  E78.G73G589 2010
  398.2089'97--dc22

                                                              2009043670

Printed in China on acid-free paper
Production Date: January 2012
Plant & Location: Printed by Everbest Printing (Guangzhou, China) Co. Ltd.
Job & Batch: 104284

For information address World Wisdom, Inc.
P.O. Box 2682, Bloomington, Indiana 47402-2682

www.worldwisdom.com

Foreword

Paul Goble and I have corresponded for almost twenty years. I use his books in the classroom and Paul periodically calls me to ask the best way to translate different Lakota words into English.

When thinking of Paul Goble, most people remember his artwork which captures the spirit of our traditional dress and camp life. But what I admire most is that he is the only non-Indian I know who has kept a Lakota flavor in his thought, in his stories. He doesn't westernize the words and he has not watered down the stories to cater to non-Indians. More than a decade ago I even translated his book, *Buffalo Woman*, into Lakota so that our Sioux people can hear his storytelling. He tells his stories as if we were sitting around a tipi campfire in the olden-days.

Traditional storytelling is important at all stages of life. Our Indian people hear the same stories over and over; we need to hear many repetitions throughout our lives. They are entertaining when we are little kids. As teenagers we start to pick up meaning in the stories. As adults we understand different levels of meaning. Morals are hidden within the stories; we learn by watching the different behaviors of people and animals in each story. Honesty, for example, is clearly shown in many behaviors. But there are also negative and disturbing aspects of many stories. In this way we learn about dishonesty. We need to hear them over and over in order to understand the deepest meanings.

I still remember as a child hearing stories of the ducks, of Iktomi (the spider), and of the woman who turned into a horse. One of my granddaughters is 4 or 5 years old and she really likes to hear these stories. One of her little friends said to her that she always thinks of the story of the woman who turned into a horse. My granddaughter told her friend that she needs to be careful or she might turn into a horse!

That's how we use the stories in different stages of our lives. They help us understand life. Stories bring out the fact that Creation has two sides— both good and bad. The morals of the stories make you look at yourself and ask the important question: which side am I on?

In 2007 Paul Goble and I sat next to each other for several hours in a bookstore while I signed my book, *Reading and Writing the Lakota Language*, and Paul signed several of his books. I asked him to come to the Hollow Horn Bear Sun Dance on the Rosebud Reservation, where I live, the following summer. As soon as Paul and his wife, Janet, arrived at the Sun Dance the next July, I had them take off their shoes and I brought them to the center pole in the middle of the sacred circle. They stood on a buffalo robe while I announced that I was honoring him for the work he has done in preserving the traditional culture of our people and then I tied a feather into his hair.

I also want to publicly honor Paul with this short Foreword. *The Boy and His Mud Horses* contains a good selection of stories that will help people at every stage of their lives. I pray that the words and illustrations in this book will reach into people's hearts and help them to better understand their place in Creation. *Heċetu welo.*

Albert White Hat, Lakota Sioux

Author's Note

From a young age I read everything I could about Native Americans, their history and material culture, but their myths and legends did not have the same interest. The problem, I later realized, is that oral literature does not "translate" well into printed words; the stories I found in books had been taken down more or less word for word from the storyteller in the oral tradition, but written they seemed to ramble on interminably, and when the gulf that exists between the two cultures is added, you have a recipe for sighs and yawns. Most material culture experts who know every detail of quill and beadwork, hardly concern themselves with the myths and yet to know a traditional culture it is necessary to have insight into their beliefs. Myths and legends are the soul of the culture.

Upon first reading, some myths seem quite prosaic, even trivial, others puzzling, but as the Pawnee, Coming Sun, told Natalie Curtis around 1900 when questioned about the meaning of a myth: "That is for each to think out for himself." We have to meditate upon their inner truths, the *ideas within.* They need to be read like stories in the Old Testament, even Gospel stories, with a different mindset than most reading. The mind has to find a place where there is no barrier between "fact" and "fantasy," where miracles and symbols live comfortably.

When I was young I listened to old Indian people who had grown up during the early reservation days, brought up by parents and grandparents who had lived during the Buffalo Days. Their conversation drifted in and out of "reality," and in listening it was often impossible to sort out what was "real" from "imaginary." I learned not to try, because who really knows where the dividing line is, or even whether there is one?

The stories here were mostly recorded during the period 1890 to 1920, few of which are in circulation today. I have not told them as Indian people during the Buffalo Days would have done, but have tried to write them in a way that can be easily read, very much shorter, making up nothing, and avoiding obscure aspects of the culture which need explanation.

* * * * * * * *

Most stories were told after dark in wintertime. Imagine, dear readers and listeners, that you are sitting on buffalo robes in the tipi, with the fire at the center casting flickering shadows on the painted lining behind you. Someone places a glowing coal in front of the storyteller, who sprinkles juniper leaves on it, filling the lodge with scent, which pleases the good spirits. He rubs his hands in the smoke, and passing them over his head and body, he purifies himself. The Star People looking down through the smoke hole will be witness to the truth of the stories he will tell . . .

Pawnee

The Boy and His Mud Horses

In ancient times the Pawnee people did not have horses, only dogs helped them carry everything they needed.

There was a poor boy in the village. He had no mother or father, nobody he could call his family. He would go from one lodge to another asking for something to eat. Many turned him away, others pretended not to notice.

Sometimes he went to the chief's lodge. The chief was kind. He felt the misery of the poor boy, and was sad to see him hungry and poorly clothed. He asked the women to give the boy food, as for an honored guest. When he sent the boy away, it was always with something to wear, a fine blanket, fringed leggings, or decorated moccasins. People chided the chief: "Why waste anything nice on the boy?" But the chief would always answer: "*Tirawa* loves him. One day he may be of help to us." People laughed.

One night the boy took his blanket to a hilltop near the village.

When we lie down looking up at the stars, and we hear the rumble of far-off thunder, who can say if we fall asleep?

Suddenly there were strange and magnificent animals in the sky, prancing hither and thither, back and forth. Thunder and lightning were in their legs, and hair on their necks and tails were swirling clouds. "Horses! These will be yours!" a voice said. "Look after them and they will carry you far."

The boy awoke. The wondrous animals were not there, and he felt terribly sad.

Before anyone was awake, he went to the river bank where there were clays of many colors: red, yellow, blue, black, and white. He shaped and smoothed, and lovingly molded the mud, keeping in his mind's eye the wonderful animals he had seen in the sky. "Horses!" the voice had called them. "All these will be yours." He made mud horses of every pattern and color, just as he had seen.

Every morning he took his mud horses to drink at the river. "Look after them," the voice said, "and they will carry you far." He loved them. They were his family. He took them from one pasture to another, looking for the choicest grass, the sweetest flowers. When evening came, he laid them down for the night in the shelter of bushes.

Another night the boy went to the hilltop, hoping to see the riders in the sky once more.

Hearing distant thunder drumming, who knows whether we dream?

The drumming grew louder and louder and everything, everywhere, was rushing wind and rain and flashing lightning. Despite the din, he heard singing, and again the voice: "Your horses are waiting! Now, this night!"

The boy ran down to where he had left his mud horses. There, standing in the moonlight and shadows, looking at him with glistening eyes and pointed ears, were real living horses. Neighing their joyful greetings they gathered around him, nudging, sniffing with their soft noses.

When the poor boy rode proudly into the village at the head of his horses, he was singing the song he had heard on the hilltop:

> *What are these coming?*
> *These, what are they?*
> *Horses!*
> *You need not fear them.*

People were excited and afraid, but the boy told them: "*Tirawa* has given us these lovely useful animals. They are called horses. Look after them and they will carry you and your packs."

The poor boy had brought a precious gift to the people, just as the chief had foretold.

Legend tells they were the first horses the Pawnees ever saw.

Cheyenne

Only the Stones Stay on Earth Forever

In sickness, or before going into battle, or facing any of life's greatest tests, people strengthened themselves with the song:

> *My friends,*
> *Only the stones*
> *Stay on earth forever.*
> *Use your best ability.*

Mandan

The Hunter and the Deer

In ancient times people dug pitfalls to trap animals for food. One day a man found a deer caught in his trap. He took an arrow from his quiver, and as he bent his bow to shoot, the deer spoke, "Don't shoot!" When the man hesitated, again the deer said, "Don't shoot!" And as the man wondered, wavering, tightening his arrow against the bowstring, again, a third time, the deer commanded him, "Don't shoot!" Then the man knew that the deer was holy.

"If you kill me," the deer said, "you will have food for only a few days, but if you let me go, I will give you my protection for all your life." Immediately the man dropped his bow and arrows, and pulled the deer out of the pit. He brushed off the dirt, and told her that she was free. The deer walked slowly away, her legs stiff from lying so long in the trap. And then she turned and said to the hunter: "I give you this song," and she sang:

> *I love that day,*
> *The first snowstorm.*
> *I am happy*
> *Again to see that day!*

Blackfoot

The Crow Lodge

There was a brave man in the Blackfoot village who had many horses which he had captured from the enemies of his people. Time and again he returned home driving a herd of horses, most of which he gave away. He had a reputation for success and the young men, too, wanted to join his war parties to capture horses.

The man's prestige and popularity grew to the point that the head man of the village became jealous. Fearing for his position as the village leader, he secretly cast spells of the blackest magic to bring the man bad luck.

Three times after that, the man returned home afoot without horses, and alone, for even his young followers had deserted him in disgust.

On his return home on foot yet a fourth time, alone and hungry, the man killed a buffalo for his meal. He made a fire to cook his meat. Afterwards he cut part of the meat into strips for his meals on his long journey home. The rest of the meat he gave as an offering to the birds and animals.

After the man had finished his work he lay down, and fell asleep. He had a dream in which a man came to him and said: "My son, I feel sad to see you walking home yet again. Like you, we too have to travel great distances when looking for our food. Because you were generous just now, giving meat to me and my children, the crows, I want to give you the design of my tipi which you are sleeping in. It is the Crow Lodge. Look carefully, and make one just like it when you get home. Keep a fire burning inside, and purify yourself each morning and evening with the smoke of burning sweet grass. I am also giving you the power to soon become the leader of your people. Now, when you awake, you will soon come across a band of horses; they will carry you home."

The man awoke, hearing shouting. He listened, and then realized it was a crow *caw-caw-cawing!*

Lakota

The False Husband

One springtime a young man and wife took down their tipi, and packing everything on their dogs, they left the village. The wife needed deer skins to make new clothes. After a short distance they again pitched their tipi, among some cottonwood trees by the river.

Early each morning the man went out to hunt, and would return before evening. The days passed, and then on one occasion it was already dark when his wife heard him return with meat and skins. He put them down outside the tipi, and threw meat to the dogs which were barking. Knowing how tired he would be after such a long day, she told him to come inside and lie down, while she went out to cover the meat for the night.

When she came back inside, and was taking off his moccasins to rest his tired feet, she felt the big toe of his left foot was missing. She was terrified: the man was not her husband! She was alone, far from any help. He was surely an enemy, but chattering still, as to her husband, she told him she would just go out and close the smoke flaps. "The night may be cool," she told him. "Go to sleep now. I'll be with you right away."

As she was adjusting the smoke flap poles, wondering which way to run, she heard the man snoring, sleeping. Taking her knife from her belt, she stole back into the lodge. She slashed once at his throat, dashed out and fled blindly away into the darkness.

At first light she found her village, and told what had happened. People rushed to see; they found the man dead, an enemy, his throat cut. He had killed the woman's husband, and had changed clothes trying to trick her, but was himself tricked, fatally.

Perhaps the woman married again. Almost certainly her husband would not have painted her brave deed, like the illustration here, because men only painted their own brave deeds; and women painted only geometric designs. Even so, a painting on skin lasts but a few years, whereas the memory of this woman's bravery has been remembered for possibly hundreds of years.

Osage
Creation Story

Generations ago, beyond counting, the Osage people lived in the sky, together with the birds and animals. Their people wondered, and asked each other: "How did we get here? Who made us? Who gave us life?"

They traveled to the Sun, and asked him. He told them they were all his children. They went to the Moon and asked her. She told them she was their mother, and the Sun, their father. She said they must leave the sky, and go down and live on the earth.

When the people reached the earth, they found it covered with water. They could not go back to the sky, and together with the birds and animals, they floated in the air above the water. They knew Elk was the strongest of them all, that he was the bravest, the most magnificent and holy, and they appealed to him for help.

Elk sank into the water, and as he swam here and there, he called upon the winds, and the Four Winds answered, blowing from every quarter of the earth. Slowly the water rose into the sky as clouds and mist. At first only rocks appeared above the water; then earth. Yet there was nothing living anywhere, nothing to eat. But Elk was so happy to rest on dry land at last, that he lay down and rolled and rolled, backwards and forwards, over and over, and wherever his hairs stuck to the earth, beans and corn grew. Squash, prairie turnips, and buffalo grass appeared, yuccas, cactus, and at the last cedars, pine trees, and mighty cottonwoods.

Those who consider
themselves beautiful
after seeing me,
have no heart.

Elk's song by
Two Shields,
Lakota.

The Dance of the Buffaloes

It was a time when the hunters could not find the buffalo herds. Everyone was hungry. There was a girl in the village who saw that her parents were not eating so that she and her brothers would have food. She was sad that she did not know how to help.

Early one morning she went to the river to fetch water. While filling her pail she was overjoyed to see a herd of buffalo on the other side of the river. "Oh!" she exclaimed. "If you will just wait until I tell the hunters, I will marry one of you!" She ran home and pointed to the buffalo. The hunters caught their fastest horses and galloped out. After that there was laughter in the village once again, with feasting admist the plenty.

When the girl went again to fetch water, a man confronted her. "Come," he said, wrapping her in his robe. "No!" she cried. "But you said you would marry one of us," and so he led her away. When they approached a herd of buffalo, she saw that he was really a buffalo, and that he was their chief.

People worried when the girl did not return. Her father searched, and while resting by a pool where the buffalo liked to drink, he noticed Magpie. "Magpie," he said, "you are a holy bird; our Father Above gave you a good mind. Help me find my daughter."

Magpie flew off and soon spotted the girl among the buffalo. They were lying down, hot and tired. Magpie landed on the great buffalo bull's back, and gently pecked at all the ticklish places which he could not reach, and soon he was asleep. "Your father waits by the pond," whispered Magpie. "Sh-h-h-h-," the girl cautioned. "Tell my father he must not move."

Soon the buffalo awoke, and the great bull told the girl to bring him a drink. She took a horn cup and went to the pond. "You must not stay here," the girl told her father. "If the buffalo see you they will surely kill you." Her father told her they should run. "No!" she said. "They will chase and kill us. Wait here until they are asleep, and then we will try to get away."

She gave the cup to the bull. Suddenly he stopped drinking and rose up. "Ha! I smell a two-legged person!" he bellowed, whipping his back with his tail. Immediately all the buffalo stood up and pawed the earth into clouds of dust. They found the man and trampled him until there was not a stain of his blood left. The girl cried. "You mourn for your father," the buffalo chief said. "Now you know how it is for us when your people kill our fathers and mothers, brothers and sisters. But I am sad to see you cry; if you can bring your father back to life, you can both go home."

The girl begged Magpie to search for anything he could find of her father. Magpie flew around, and returned with a single bone from the man's back. The girl put it on the ground, and covered it with her blanket. When she lifted the blanket, her father was lying there, asleep. She spread the blanket again, and pulling it away, her father awoke. "Ah-h-h-h-!" exclaimed the buffaloes in amazement. Magpie flew around making joyful calls.

The buffalo chief spoke: "Today we have seen wonderful things: two-legged people have mysterious powers. Before you go back to your people, hear our songs," and the buffaloes sang, and they danced in a circle around the girl and her father. "Go home," the great buffalo told them, "remember our songs, and dance. Teach them to your people, and when you are hungry and cannot find us, dance, and we will hear, and we will come to you."

Cheyenne

Matama's Gift of the Buffalo and Corn

The people were camped in a large circle. At the circle's entrance there was a little hill, below which was a deep spring called Matama Hehkait, Old Woman's Water.

There was no food and everyone was hungry. One morning a crowd gathered at the center of the circle to watch a game. They were gambling on its outcome, when a young man came from the south side of the circle and stood behind the crowd to watch. He was wearing a buffalo robe, and was painted yellow all over, with a yellow painted eagle breath-feather tied in his hair.

Soon another young man, dressed exactly the same as the other, came from the opposite side of the circle to watch. Their names were Standing on the Ground and Sweet Root Standing. They were both surprised when they saw they were dressed alike. "Friend," one said, "why do you imitate me?" The game stopped and everyone listened. "No, friend," the other replied, "why do you imitate me? Mine is sacred paint. When I went into Matama's Water I was told to paint myself like this." The other said that he, too, received his paint from the spring. "Then let us both go, together, and do this special thing for everyone." They told the crowds, "This very day we will bring you something wonderful which will make you happy," and they walked to the spring, covered their heads with their robes, and plunged in.

They went through the spring, and entered a cave underneath the little hill where Matama, the Old Woman, lived. "Come in, Grandsons, and sit beside me," she told them, and she held each in her arms for a while. "Why did you not come sooner, my Grandchildren? Why have you gone hungry for so long?" She put two wooden bowls before them, one filled with cooked buffalo meat, and the other with corn. They ate fast because they were hungry, but as much as they ate, the bowls remained full.

When they had eaten, Matama pointed to the north. "Look that way!" she said, and they looked, and everywhere the land was black with buffalo herds. "Look that way!" she said, pointing to the south, and there were immense fields of ripening corn waving in the breeze. "All this will be food for your people," she told them. "At sunset I will let out the buffalo. Take this uncooked corn in your robes and plant it in moist ground."

As the young men stepped out of the spring, they saw that their bodies were painted red, and that each wore a red breath-feather in his hair. When the people saw that they were bringing food, they sat in a line waiting. Standing on the Ground brought the bowl of corn, and Sweet Root Standing the bowl of buffalo meat. As much as the people ate, the bowls remained full, but at the last, the poor and orphaned children ate until the bowls were empty.

At sunset everyone watched the spring. Suddenly a young buffalo bull jumped out. He played, and rolled in the mud, and then he jumped back in again. Soon another sprang out, and then more, and soon they came out so fast that nobody could ever keep count. They poured out all night, and the ground shook with the thunder of their hooves. When the sun came up, the land was black with grazing buffalo in every direction.

In the spring everyone moved to lower ground, close to a river where they planted the corn in moist earth. Matama had given the people both corn and buffalo, and they were no longer hungry.

Lakota and Arikara

The Legend of Standing Rock

There was a young man in the Arikara village who returned home one day from a war expedition against the Grosventre enemy. He rode around the village, leading a girl on another horse, while announcing in a loud voice how he had captured her from the Grosventre people, and was now taking her for his second wife.

His first wife saw at once that her husband had eyes only for this girl, and the next morning when the village struck their tipis and moved away, she left and climbed to the top of a hill. She was so unhappy that she just sat with her blanket around her covering her face, and refused to move or speak to anyone. The people rode away, leaving her on the hilltop, her favorite dog lying beside her.

There was a thunderstorm during the night and the man worried for his wife left behind. The next morning when she had still not caught up with the village, he asked his brothers to go back for her. "Such a night alone on the hill will have brought your sister-in-law to her senses," he assured them. "Tell the woman to come back." They found her, still sitting on the hilltop, her blanket drawn over her head, the dog beside her. When she would not speak, one of the brothers touched her cheek, but immediately withdrew his hand. "Our sister-in-law has turned into stone!" he whispered. *"Stone?"* *"Stone."*

They hurried back to tell their brother, and the whole village came to see. The rock was *lila wakan*, very mysterious, sacred.

Men have said that the story is a reminder to wives that they must follow their husbands. Women, on the other hand, have felt sadness and pity, and over the years those with difficulties in their marriages have talked to the rock seeking advise, and been comforted. In gratitude some have left food and offerings, while others have daubed sacred vermilion paint on the rock.

Indian people call it the Standing Rock. It has power to help people, they say. And then one day a white building contractor, searching for stones, carried away the woman and her dog for his work, and threw them among a pile of other rocks he had collected. The dog rock looked so much like others that it was never found, but the woman rock was easily identified by its splashes of vermilion paint, and today it stands on a pedestal outside the Hunkpapa Tribal Office on the Standing Rock Indian Reservation at Fort Yates, North Dakota.

Mandan

The Eagle and the Jackrabbit

A young man was sitting on a lonely hilltop wrapped in his blanket. Like all men, he was there to fast, and to pray to the Great Spirit to give him a helper for his path through life. The helper might be Crow or Badger, Buffalo or Antelope, perhaps the smallest of the birds or animals, even an insect.

While he sat on the hilltop the young man observed an Eagle chasing a Jackrabbit. Suddenly the Jackrabbit turned and ran up to him and jumped into the folds of his blanket. "Save me!" the Jackrabbit pleaded, "and I will be your helper to guide you always."

After that the man grew in wisdom, they say, and was honored by his people.

I include this incidental story because a jackrabbit, which was being chased by a dog, dashed up to me, knowing I would turn the dog away. Birds and animals observe us without us knowing.

Blackfoot and Many Nations

Kutoyis Captured the Snake Lodge

An old man and his wife had three daughters who were married to the same man. The old people lived on their own. Their son-in-law was very mean to them. He would make the old man butcher the buffalo he killed, but would never let him take home any meat. Only when the son-in-law was not looking could his wives sneak a little meat for their parents.

One day when the old man had been butchering, and was again returning home without any meat, he spotted a big clot of blood in the grass. Pretending to fall down, spilling the arrows out of his quiver, he quickly dropped the blood-clot into his quiver. "What are you doing, old man?" shouted his son-in-law. The old man said that he was just picking up his arrows which had spilled. "You're a good for nothing lazy old man."

The moment the old man got home, he whispered to his wife: "Build up the fire. Tonight we shall have blood soup!" As the water started to heat, they heard crying coming from inside the pot. Looking inside there was a tiny baby boy with outstretched arms in the water! The old woman rushed and took him out, and wrapped him up. The son-in-law heard the crying. "The old woman has had another baby! If it's a boy I'll kill it." He sent his wives to find out, but they told him it was a girl. He was happy; he could look forward to yet another wife one day.

The old people called the baby Kutoyis, Blood-Clot, and that night the baby boy spoke: "Take me up, my Father and my Mother, and touch me to each of the tipi poles in turn." Surprised by such a request, they did so, and with each succeeding pole the boy became heavier to carry, and when they touched him to the last pole he stood, a handsome young man. "I am hungry," he told them. "Why is there nothing here to eat?" Then they told him how their son-in-law kept all the food. "We live on the little that our daughters are able to steal for us."

Kutoyis killed the evil son-in-law. "Now my work here is done," he told them. "I must leave you. I am Smoking Star, the Comet; I travel from place to place looking for people who need my help."

Kutoyis set out on his travels and came to a fine tall painted tipi. Beside it was pitched a small lodge with a worn-out cover, and he knew that only very poor people would live in such a lodge. He entered and found it belonged to two old women. They gave him dried meat to eat, but Kutoyis asked, "Why do you give me these scraps of dried meat, with no fat or berries?" "Hush. . . !" the old women cautioned him, "if you speak so loud the snakes who live in the big lodge will hear you, and they will eat you. They keep all the best food for themselves, and all we have are the scraps they don't eat."

When he had finished eating he told the women that he would go to the snakes' lodge and have some more to eat. "No, don't go!" they pleaded, "they will surely kill you." But Kutoyis was angry.

The snakes were all sleeping when he entered the lodge, and he helped himself to some berry soup. "Wake up!" he called out, and he pricked the chief snake with his white stone knife. Instantly the snake awoke and tried to strike, but with one swish of his knife, Kutoyis cut off its head. Then he killed all the snakes, except for one who was about to become a mother, which slipped away underneath the lodge cover.

Kutoyis gave the women the fine tipi and all the food which was stored in it. He than set out on his travels once again to look for other people who needed his help. And he travels still, today. . .

Every snake in the world today is a descendant of the snake which Kutoyis allowed to escape. His capture of the Snake Lodge is only one of the many exploits in the oral tradition of the Buffalo Days, told on and on during the long winter evenings. He conquered mystic bears, man-eaters, dangerous women, and the fearful Wind Sucker. All Nations have their Savior: he is always young and handsome, and he never ages. He is called by different names: Falling Star, Stone Boy, Lodge Boy, White Plume Boy.

The snake-painted tipi is still with the Blackfoot people in Montana and Alberta. Two snakes circle the tipi, their heads toward the door; the male snake, with the one horn on his head, is always painted on the south side of the lodge cover (tipis always face east), the female snake painted on the north side. A painted circle above the tipi's door represents the snakes' den.

Cheyenne

The Stolen Girl

This is a story about Pack Rats, but do not imagine, dear readers, that Pack Rats are anything like the rats of cities and farms. Correctly called Bushey-tailed Woodrats, they live only in the high country among the trees, where they make enormous nests of things they collect, or steal: twigs, grass, and these days even plastic, paper cups, or candy wrappers, and just about anything small that campers leave unguarded.

The writer of these lines once rented a car and went camping in the mountains. A pair of Pack Rats decided that the car would be a fine place to make a nest. During the night they took out much of the upholstery foam from the back seat cushions, and stuffed it into the heating and air-conditioning pipes. When discovered, it seemed almost heartless to persuade them to leave; they looked so appealing with their soft gray fur and beautiful large nocturnal red eyes. . .

Many of the young men in the village had wanted to marry the chief's beautiful daughter. She could have chosen any one of them, but she always hoped that one day she would find a young man whom she truly loved.

One evening she was lying in bed, waiting for sleep, and who can tell when sleep comes? Was she still awake, or was she already asleep when she heard the soft notes on a flute? Someone was just outside the tipi. Who could play such beautiful melodies? She needed to know, but she did not want to be seen looking out of the door. Finding her awl, she poked a hole in the tipi cover, and peeping through she saw a young man wrapped in a blanket playing his flute. As she listened, nobody had ever moved her so with joy. She went outside the tipi as if to set the smoke flap poles against a change in the wind, and when passing, he wrapped her in his blanket. "I have come for you," he told her. "Come with me and I will take you to my father's lodge." The girl replied: "Other young men want me, but I will go only with you. But first I must go back and collect my work things," and she bundled up her awl and sinew and her bags of colored porcupine quills.

"Now I am ready," she told him, and he led her away from the camp. "What do people call you?" she asked, and he replied: "They call me Red Eye." Soon they came to the young man's tipi among the trees. There were many people inside; she could see their shadows through the tipi cover where they sat around the fire.

A man was saying: "My son has gone to woo a chief's daughter. He wants to marry her. He hopes to bring her here tonight." Red Eye led the girl into the tipi and she sat on the women's side. The lodge was nicely furnished with linings and pillows beautifully embroidered with colored porcupine quills. The beds were warm buffalo robes. Red Eye was speaking to his father, and for the first time the girl noticed that they both had very sharp noses, and looking around the lodge she saw that they all had sharp noses.

Back at the girl's home the next morning everyone was upset that the chief's daughter had vanished. The chief told the young men: "Go and look for my daughter. Search everywhere!"

When the girl awoke, she found that she was inside a hollow tree, and sitting around the tree were Pack Rats. The pillows and linings were cobwebs and rotting wood, and the buffalo robe beds were only grass nests.

A young man from the villlage found her. "Why are you here?" he asked. "Everyone is worried, looking for you." "Friend," the girl replied, "the Pack Rats stole me and brought me here." So it was, they say, that Pack Rats first started stealing things from people.

Cheyenne
The Bat

*This story and the story which follows, **The Frogs and the Bull Snake**, are examples of little stories which mothers told their children to put them to sleep. They were stories about familiar animals: bats, frogs, chipmunks, or mice who sometimes stole food from mother's rawhide cases, or the little ground squirrels whose underground homes were everywhere around the tipis at some campgrounds. Like nursery rhymes, the stories were told over and over so the children knew them by heart, and while listening, they were soon fast asleep.*

Bat had been awake all night. Now, at daylight, he was asleep, hanging upside-down among the rocks. Bobcat, who was hunting, caught Bat in his claws. "Please don't eat me!" pleaded Bat. "Let's be friends! I'm an animal just like you. See, I have fur, even teeth and ears." Bobcat thought about it: he let Bat go.

Bat had been asleep all day. Now, at nightfall, he was flying around, hunting for a moth to eat. Owl, who was also hunting, caught Bat in his talons. "Please don't eat me!" pleaded Bat. "Let's be friends! I'm a bird just like you. See, I have wings." Owl thought about it: he let Bat go.

Birds and animals can never quite make up their minds whether or not Bat is one of them. Bat is happy to leave it that way.

Cheyenne

The Frogs and the Bull Snake

One day Mother Frog was at home with her many children among the reeds at the edge of the pond, when Bull Snake suddenly appeared slithering slowly in at the side door of their happy home. "Oh my dears!" exclaimed Mother Frog. "Just look whose here! It's your Uncle, come to visit. How lovely to see you, dear Brother. Here are your nephews and nieces, all of them named after you. Hop along now, children, and quickly get some firewood so I can cook for your Uncle," but she whispered to her children, "Run for your life! He means to eat you!"

After a while Mother Frog said, "I wonder what is taking the children so long with that firewood. Excuse me a moment, dear Brother, I'll go and hurry them up," and she hopped out of the door to safety with all her children.

Lakota
The Girl and the Wild Horses

In ancient times it was the custom for parents to choose wives and husbands for their sons and daughters, and usually everyone was happy with that arrangement. But not always: in those long gone days there was a girl who refused to marry the man her parents chose; she feared him. She was sad and cried often, but her parents were determined that she should change her mind.

On a day when the village was moving to a new campsite, the girl left the line of people and their horses which carried the tipis and belongings. She had taken her digging stick, and her mother thought she had gone to dig turnips. When evening came and her daughter had still not returned, she was worried. People rode back to look for her, and although they searched, they never found her.

Years later when hunters came again to the same part of the country, they saw a herd of wild horses coming out of a cave, followed by a strange and beautiful woman with two colts and a magnificent stallion. The hunters watched. When the horses had been to drink at the river and had grazed, they went back into the cave. The hunters wondered whether it was the girl who had been lost. They watched, together with the girl's parents for two more days, and each day it was the same. The parents knew it was their daughter.

On the fourth day the men gathered, riding their fastest horses. After the wild horses had their drink at the river, the riders galloped down upon them. The woman, leading the colts, tried to get away, but when she could not keep up with the herd, she let the colts go. Although the stallion stayed back to defend her, he could not help. She begged for her freedom: "The stallion is my husband and the colts my children. If you let me go, I will live forever. If you keep me, I will die." For many days the stallion and the colts followed the people at a distance, calling, calling. And then one day they did not come again. The woman pleaded, but her parents never understood, and she died when still a young woman.

Navaho

My Horse Song

My horse is slim like a weasel!
My horse has a hoof like a striped agate.
His fetlock is like a fine eagle plume.
His legs are like quick lightning.
My horse's body is like an eagle-plumed arrow.
My horse has a tail like a trailing black cloud.
The little holy wind blows through his hair.
His mane is made of short rainbows.
My horse's ears are made like round corn.
My horse's eyes are made of big stars.
My horse's head is made of mixed waters
From the holy waters, he never knows thirst.
My horse's teeth are made of white shell.
The long rainbow is in his mouth for a bridle,
And with it I guide him.
When my horse neighs, different colored horses follow.
I am wealthy because of him!

Lakota

The Lost Baby

A young mother left the village and walked out on to the prairie to dig turnips, *timpsila*. She carried her digging stick and her baby wrapped in its soft beaded cradle. When she came to where the turnips grew, she laid down her baby in the tall grass. She worked hard digging up the roots and gathering them into a bag tied around her waist. Searching here and there among the grass for the blue-flowered *timpsila*, she worked for quite a long time.

When she walked back to feed her baby, it was not where she thought she had left it. The prairie looked the same in every direction, the grass everywhere rippling like a lake in the wind. She walked here, there, searching, but she could not find her baby. She listened for its cry, perhaps, but still it was only the grasshoppers calling to each other.

Searching frantically hither and thither, at last she heard a cry and glimpsed something moving. She ran to pick up her precious baby, but instead a Sandpiper flew up into the air with a sad crying call like a baby.

Her relatives found her there crying. The baby was never found. When people heard the sad call of the Upland Sandpiper they knew the baby had been mysteriously changed into one of the Bird People, and taken up into the sky.

Sometimes on still, warm nights in Spring, the bird's whimpering cry could be heard; people would say it was the lost baby's cry.

Mandan

Coyote and Skunk Go Hunting

One day Coyote and Skunk were walking along together. Skunk was dressed in his black and white striped clothes, while Coyote had dressed himself to look like a little wolf. Coyote said to Skunk that he was hungry, and Skunk said that he, too, was hungry.

Between them they hatched a plan to catch some Prairie Dogs to eat. Coyote cut pieces of hollow reeds, and hung them by strings from Skunk's striped ears and tail. Skunk danced, rattling his hollow reeds, while Coyote sang and beat upon a drum.

"Oh look!" the Prairie Dogs exclaimed. "It's Coyote and Skunk dancing! Let's go and see!" They left the doorways of their underground houses, and ran and joined in the dancing. Skunk shook and rattled the reeds tied to his ears and tail, while Coyote beat ever louder and louder on his drum, singing about Skunk:

> *My face is striped*
> *My back is striped*
> *My tail rattles*
> *My ears rattle*
> *Each end rattles*
> *My whole body rattles*

All the while they drew the Prairie Dogs ever farther and farther from the safety of their underground homes.

Every young girl in the Mandan village knew the story well, and how it ended. They grew up singing Skunk's song. They would sing it as they danced in a line, one behind the other, each holding on to the dress of the girl in front, singing and dancing, round and round the village.

Blackfoot

The All Star Lodge

Day after day a man left home to look for the buffalo, but they were nowhere to be found, and each evening he returned home empty-handed.

Before leaving one morning, he told his wife: "If I do not find the buffalo today, I will sleep wherever night overtakes me. I will not return until I can bring some meat for you and the children."

When darkness came he found a sheltered place to sleep. During the night he dreamed he met a man who told him: "My Son, I know that you and your wife and children are hungry. I feel sorry for you, searching and searching but finding nothing. You are right among the buffalo herds and yet you cannot see them! Tomorrow you will take home all the meat you can carry, but come now to my lodge and eat with me." The man led the way to a painted lodge, which had one side painted red, the other side yellow, and with white stars all over.

After they had eaten, the man said: "My Son, I want to give you my lodge. You think these are stars painted on it, but they are not stars at all, they are buffalo dung! Look at it carefully, and when you get home copy it. Then you will never again have to search for the buffalo; you will always be right among them! You and your family will never be hungry again."

The lodge design has been passed down through many generations, and always those who live in it have good luck and are never without meat.

Blackfoot
Peace with the Shoshones

Owl Bear, the loved and respected leader of his people, awoke one morning from a good dream. Excited to tell it, he called everyone together: "I had a strong dream," he told them, "that we captured many horses from our Shoshone enemies. It is a good omen. Who will go with me?" The young men were eager, and they say that Owl Bear went to war leading more than two hundred warriors.

They traveled on foot over the mountains toward the country of the Shoshones. The first night away from home some men had bad dreams, seeing themselves badly wounded, dying. When they had similar dreams the following night, many lost confidence. "Go home!" Owl Bear derided. "I don't want cowards. Go back!"

Only his close relatives stayed, and they, too, wanted to turn back. "It is bad luck to go on," they told him. "Too many dreams warn us something bad will surely happen." Then Owl Bear became angry: "Even you, my own relatives, call yourselves warriors. Go home! And when you get back to your wives, put on women's clothes."

After that Owl Bear was left alone, dejected that everyone had deserted him. He did not want to live. It was starting to rain and he looked for somewhere dry. Finding a cave among the rocks, he crept inside. Feeling his way in the dark to the back, he suddenly put his hand on a leg. He hesitated, then felt again . . . yes, a man's leg! Neither man spoke, but by feeling and signs, and a few words, Owl Bear knew the other was an enemy, a Shoshone. He told the Shoshone that his people had deserted him, and that he no longer wanted to live. He drew his knife and put it in the right hand of the Shoshone, wrapping the man's fingers around the handle.

Owl Bear expected to die, but as he waited for the blow, the Shoshone placed his own knife into Owl Bear's hand, and said, "Like you, I was leading my people but now they have left me, and I, too, wanted to die. But let us not fight. Instead let us smoke the pipe, and then bring our two nations together in friendship."

So it was, they say, that the two nations, who had always been enemies, pitched their tipis together, and made peace. There was dancing and feasting, and generous gifts were exchanged. After the two peoples had camped happily for many days, each left for its own hunting grounds.

A few young men stayed behind for a while to gamble and to race their horses. A quarrel broke out about the winner, and soon they started to shoot, and people were killed.

No peace between the Blackfoot and the Shoshones ever lasted.

Dakota and Lakota
Blood Turned to Stone

For Native American peoples the sacred pipe, often called the peace pipe, is a portable altar, and a means to commune with God; prayers visibly rise to heaven with the pipe's smoke. Pipes have been made of different kinds of stone, but the most desirable has always been the red pipestone found at the Pipestone Quarry in western Minnesota, close to the South Dakota border. Today the stone is called Catlinite, named after George Catlin, who was an early visitor to the quarry in the 1830s.

In ancient times the quarry was a place of peaceful pilgrimage where people obtained stone for their pipes. Tradition tells it was the place where the Great Spirit came down to earth, seeking peace between warlike humankind. Standing on the high cliff above the quarry, he told them to smoke the pipe of peace together. Henry Wadsworth Longfellow captured the spirit of this tradition in his poem The Song of Hiawatha. *Today the quarry is a National Monument, and Indian people still quarry stone. In Catlin's day white people were unwelcome, and he was warned: "This pipestone is part of our flesh. The red men are part of the red stone. If the white men take away a piece of the red pipestone, it is a hole in our flesh, and the blood will always run. We cannot stop the blood from running."*

It is told why pipestone is part of the flesh of Indian people:
Long, long ago, they say, there was a world just like our world, but one day the Creator decided to destroy it. Perhaps people were living bad lives, and he was angry with them. He made it rain and rain, day after day, and everywhere the water rose and rose until it covered everything. There was just one high cliff on the prairies

which remained above the water. Crowds of people gathered there, they say, hoping to be saved, but even there, little by little the waters rose. When there was no room left for them all to stand, the Four Winds blew, and great waves broke over the cliff top, and the people were swept away and drowned.

Tradition tells that their bodies sank to the base of that high cliff, and there the Creator turned their bodies and blood into the holy red stone.

Out of the old world grew a new world, our world. No one knows how many generations came and were forgotten, but it was the Buffalo Nation who first showed people where to find the sacred red stone, the blood of their ancestors.

Buffaloes make well-worn paths as they walk from one grassland or river to another. People, too, found the buffalo paths the easiest way to travel from one place to another. Walking to and fro beneath the high cliff, the buffaloes uncovered the beautiful red stone. There, people found it, washed and polished by wind and rain, and by the hooves of the Buffalo People.

Pipes are still made with this red stone. All these mysteries, dear readers and listeners, were born in the imagination of the Great Spirit, the Creator, God.

The Buffalo Rocks

It was spring, and a time of famine. Everyone in the village had shared their last food. They were weak with hunger. The Buffalo People had quite deserted them. The village elders asked the young men who were still strong to go out, and only to return when they had found meat for the women and children, and the old people.

On the fourth day the hunters saw in the distance a group of buffaloes lying down. The hunters quickly got out of sight. Two who were known to be the best hunters were chosen to go forward and to kill two of the buffaloes. They crept towards the animals, and when close, they saw that a group of buffalo cows were sitting around a large bull. All were sleeping. When in range of their arrows, still the buffaloes were not moving, not a tail twitched, not an ear flicked. At first the hunters just lay there looking at the buffaloes, but then at each other. Something was happening which they could not understand. They stood up and beckoned to their comrades to come. The buffaloes had turned into stone.

Their leader spoke: "It is always when we are far away from home, away from people and chatter, that we see strange and wonderful things. This place is sacred. The Buffalo Spirits are here. Let us unwrap and fill the pipe, and see our prayers rise up in the smoke. We will pray that the Buffalo Spirits will look kindly on us, and give us food."

Afterwards they cleaned and wrapped the pipe again, and as they prepared to resume their search, they saw that the view to the south was black with returning multitudes of the Buffalo Nation.

When white people first came to the prairies they found that the boulders were covered with red paint. There were offerings scattered everywhere: pipes, beautiful quill work, knives, bows and arrows, eagle feathers and other things of value. Whenever Indian people passed the Buffalo Rocks, they would offer prayers, for good hunting, or for strength in old age, for good health for their families, or that the people would be happy and have many horses.

Lakota and Arapaho
Buffalo Hunting Songs

Imprisoned on small reservations, and the buffalo slaughtered to near extinction, Indian people lived in despair, their way of life shattered. A new religion arose, the Ghost Dance, giving hope that the old days would return. These songs came to the dancers in dreams, songs of longing for their happy buffalo hunting days.

*From all over the earth they are coming:
A Nation is coming! A Nation is coming!
The Eagle has brought the news to the People
From all over the whole earth they are coming:
The Buffalo are coming! The Buffalo are coming!
The Crow has brought the news to the People.*

*Hey! The scouts have returned galloping.
They say there will be a Buffalo hunt over there.
Make arrows! Make arrows!*

*Give me my knife.
I will hang up meat to dry—ye ye!
Says Grandmother.
When it is dry I will make pemmican—ye ye!
Says Grandmother.*

*They are about to chase the Buffalo.
Grandmother, give me my bow.
Grandmother, give me my bow.*

*Father, give me my arrows.
The Buffalo have come.
I will eat pemmican. I will eat pemmican.*

*How bright is the moonlight!
Tonight as I ride with my load of buffalo meat.*

Blackfoot and Many Nations

The Star Children

To understand this story, dear readers and listeners, it is necessary to know two things: first, that this story was told long before the Spaniards brought horses to the continent. In those days Indian peoples who lived on the Great Plains relied on their dogs to help carry their belongings when they followed the buffalo herds.

Second, you need to know that baby buffaloes, born in the earliest springtime, are specially favored: when first born their fur is red, a special kind of red which seems to glow in the sunshine. After only a week or two this red changes to a golden yellow. By late summer they are brown, just like their mothers and fathers, uncles and aunts. After the spring buffalo hunt, it was the custom for people to honor their youngest sons by giving them these little red calf robes.

In ancient times, there were six little orphan boys. Nobody cared for them; they slept and ate wherever they could. After the early spring buffalo hunt, families gave their children beautiful little red calf robes, but nobody gave anything to the orphan boys. The other children made fun of the orphans' robes, which were only tattered pieces of buffalo hide, calling them "scabby old bulls."

The orphans were ashamed. Not wanting to live with people any longer, they wandered out on the plains and climbed to a hilltop.

"Let us go up into the sky," the oldest boy said. "Shut your eyes," he told them, and blowing a little feather into the air, they were carried up into the sky. When they opened their eyes they found they were in the lodge of Sun and Moon. "My children, why have you come?" Moon asked, and the children told how they were treated badly. Moon pitied the boys, calling them "my poor boys."

She asked Sun to take away all the water from the people. He turned the grass brown, and burned the forests. The rivers and lakes dried up and the earth cracked open. Everyone was dying of thirst, but the dogs saved the people; they dug holes in the dry river banks, and spring water gushed out.

That is how springs of water began, and so people are ever grateful to their dogs.

The leader of the dogs was old and white. He howled, praying to Sun and Moon, appealing to them for pity on everyone below, to send them rain.

Dogs still howl at night, talking to Moon.

Now the boys are called the Bunched Stars (Pleiades), because they are close together, as they were on earth. You can see them, except in the spring when the buffalo calves are red, the time of their shame.

Most Blackfoot painted lodges have the Bunched Stars painted on one of the smoke flaps, reminding us of this sad story.

Blackfoot

The Woman Who Found the Buffalo Stone

One winter, long ago, before the people had horses, the buffalo had quite vanished; the dried meat in the parfleche bags had all been eaten, and everyone in the village was hungry.

When a young man, whose name was Chief Speaking, had killed a jackrabbit, he asked Weasel Woman, his wife, to cook it. She left the tipi to gather wood for the cooking fire. As she walked among the cottonwood trees by the river, picking up pieces of fire-wood, she heard a beautiful voice singing, and yet there was no singer anywhere. She listened. Again she heard the song!

> *Woman, hear me:*
> *I have great power.*
> *Woman, take me,*
> *I have great power.*

Listening carefully, she found the singing came from a crevice in a tree trunk. Inside was a little polished stone in the shape of a buffalo, nestled in shed buffalo wool. The stone spoke to her: "I am a Buffalo Stone (*Iniskim*). Take me home. Teach the people my song, and when it is dark, sing and pray that the buffalo will hear you. They will surely come back."

Weasel Woman was afraid, but she took the stone, wrapped it in the buffalo wool, and carried it inside her dress. She gave it to her husband, and she told him how she had heard the song, and had found the stone, and what it had said. She said to everyone who by this time had gathered: "The buffalo will come here tomorrow morning, but first of all, an aged bull will walk through our village tonight. You must be sure," she warned them, "that no one harms him." And then she passed the stone around and everyone kissed it. "Your hearts will be glad," she told them. "We shall have food tomorrow."

Everyone was excited, and that night when the old buffalo bull walked slowly through the village everyone was happy, because they knew that the stone had spoken truly. "Ah-a-a! Don't hurt him," they told each other. "Rub his back for him with firewood."

Daybreak came with snow from the north, and drifting slowly against the snow, came the Buffalo People, more than anyone could count, wandering right in among the tipis.

The buffalo had been drawn by the power of the stone, and after that, whenever the stone called, the buffalo would come and give themselves so that the people could live. It was the way *Napi*, the Creator, meant it to be, even from the beginning times.

The stone was wrapped in buffalo wool and always kept inside a bundle, and it was only unwrapped with prayer and ceremony when the people needed to find the buffalo. In time it was found that upon opening the bundle, the Buffalo Stone had given birth to young stones. Then other people in the village looked after their own *Iniskim*. The stones gave the people great power with the buffalo.

The Coming of the Corn

A man and woman had been married for many years, but they had no child. They prayed often, asking the Great Spirit to give them one. They sought the prayers and guidance of the holy men of the village, who took them into the purification lodge, the sweat bath. When the pipe had been smoked and water sprinkled on the red-hot rocks at the center of the lodge, a voice spoke out of the steam and heat: "Your prayers have been heard. Tomorrow you will receive what you wish."

The man and his wife were excited. The next morning, in front of the tipi door, was growing a plant they had never seen before. Not understanding what it meant, they went again to the village holy men, and again a voice out of the steam and heat was heard: "Do not be anxious. This plant will grow into the most beautiful child. Give it sunlight and water." The man and woman realized the plant was to be their child, and as good parents, they gave it water and kept it free of weeds. Their child grew tall with green clothes and fair hair, and with cobs of corn wrapped in green.

That was the first corn. In time all the people had corn. They called it Mother Corn, because, like a mother, she gives blessings of life and abundance to her children.

Black Elk, a Lakota holy man, explained the meanings of the corn:
The ear of corn has twelve important meanings, for there are twelve rows of kernels, which it receives from the various powers of the universe: our closest relatives, Grandfather and Father, Great Spirit, our Grandmother and Mother, the Earth, the four Powers of the universe, the red and blue days, the light and darkness, the Morning Star, and the Spotted Eagle who guards all that is sacred.

The tassel which grows upon the top of the ear of corn represents the presence of the Great Spirit, for, as the pollen from the tassel spreads all over, giving life, so it is with God who gives life to all things. The flower, which is at the top of the plant, is the first to see the light of dawn, and it sees also the night and moon and all the stars. The corn plant is like the tree of life, reaching from Earth to Heaven, and the fruit, which is the ear with all its kernels, represents the people and all things of the universe. For all these reasons it is very sacred.

Lakota

The Old Woman Who Lives in the Badlands

On the Great Plains there are lonely and beautiful places where colored earths are exposed, and where little grows except cactus and cedar trees. White people call these places "badlands," but they are only "bad" because white people found no use there. And that is good because somewhere in the "badlands," they say, there still lives an old woman in a tipi with her big black dog. She is older than anyone knows, perhaps as old as the buttes themselves.

Year after year, she sits in her tipi embroidering a buffalo robe with colored porcupine quills into most exquisite designs, more beautiful than any mortal can ever imagine. Her hands are white with dry clay so she does not soil the white robe, and she softens quills in her mouth before sewing them into her embroidery. All the while her old dog lies beside her, watching, always watching.

Hanging over a fire is a kettle of sweet red berry soup, *wojapi*. She puts her work down, and slowly gets up, bent with age, to make up the fire, and to stir her *wojapi*. When her back is turned, her dog quickly pulls apart the quill embroidery she has just finished. And so her work is never finished. They say that when it is finished, right then, at that very instant, the world will come to an end.

Ahhh . . . Keyapi, that's what they say.

REFERENCES

Astrov, Margot, *AMERICAN INDIAN PROSE AND POETRY*, New York: Capricorn Books, 1962. Bordeaux, William J., *CONQUERING THE MIGHTY SIOUX*, Sioux Falls: Privately published, 1929. Brown, Joseph Epes, *THE SACRED PIPE*, Norman: University of Oklahoma Press, 1953. Brown Wolf, Oliver, *THE WOMAN WHO LIVED WITH THE WOLVES*, Eagle Butte Public School, Title VII Bilingual Program, 1982. Buechel, Fr. Eugene, *LAKOTA TALES AND TEXTS*, ed. Paul Manhart, SJ, Vermillion: University of South Dakota, 1978. Curtis, Natalie, *THE INDIANS' BOOK*, New York: Harper and Brothers, 1923. Deloria, Ella, *DAKOTA TEXTS*, Vermillion: University of South Dakota, 1978. Densmore, Frances, *CHIPPEWA MUSIC*, Bureau of American Ethnology, Bulletin 45, Washington DC: Smithsonian Institution, 1910; *TETON SIOUX MUSIC*, Bureau of American Ethnology, Bulletin 61, Washington DC: Smithsonian Institution, 1918; *MANDAN AND HIDATSA MUSIC*, Bureau of American Ethnology, Bulletin 80, Washington DC: Smithsonian Institution, 1923; *PAWNEE MUSIC*, Bureau of American Ethnology, Bulletin 93, Washington DC: Smithsonian Institution, 1929. Dorsey, George A., *THE CHEYENNE INDIANS*, Vol. I, Anthropological Series, Vol. IX, No. 1, Chicago: Field Columbian Museum, 1905; *THE PAWNEE MYTHOLOGY*, Washington DC: Carnegie Institution, 1906. Dorsey, George A., and Alfred L. Kroeber, *TRADITIONS OF THE ARAPAHO*, Chicago: Field Columbian Museum, 1903. Ewers, John C., *THE HORSE IN BLACKFOOT INDIAN CULTURE*, Bureau of American Ethnology, Bulletin 159, Washington DC: Smithsonian Institution, 1955; *BLACKFOOT TIPIS, DESIGN AND LEGEND*, Bozeman: Museum of the Rockies, 1976. Gilmore, Melvin R., *PRAIRIE SMOKE*, New York: Columbia University Press, 1929. Grinnell, George Bird, *PAWNEE HERO STORIES AND FOLK TALES*, New York: Forest and Stream Publishing Co., 1889; *BLACKFOOT LODGE TALES*, New York: Charles Scribner's Sons, 1892; *THE STORY OF THE INDIAN*, London: Chapman and Hall, 1896; *SOME EARLY CHEYENNE TALES*, Journal of American Folklore, Vol. XX, No. LXXVIII, 1907; *BY CHEYENNE CAMPFIRES*, New Haven: Yale University Press, 1926; *PAWNEE, BLACKFOOT AND CHEYENNE*, New York: Charles Scribner's Sons, 1961; *THE CHEYENNE INDIANS*, New York: Cooper Square, 1962. Hungry Wolf, Beverly, *THE WAYS OF MY GRANDMOTHERS*, New York: William Morrow & Company, 1980. Hyde, George A., *LIFE OF GEORGE BENT*, Norman: University of Oklahoma Press, 1968. Kennedy, Michael Stephen, *THE ASSINBOINES*, Norman: University of Oklahoma Press, 1961. Marriott, Alice and Carol K. Rachlin, *AMERICAN INDIAN MYTHOLOGY*, New York: Thomas Y. Crowell Company, 1968. McClintock, Walter, *THE OLD NORTH TRAIL*, London: Macmillan, 1910. One Feather, Vivian, *EHANNI OHUNKAKAN*, Pine Ridge: Red Cloud Indian School, 1974. Powell, Fr. Peter J., *SWEET MEDICINE*, Norman: University of Oklahoma Press, 1969. Schultz, James Willard, *BLACKFEET AND BUFFALO*, Norman: University of Oklahoma Press, 1962. Smith, Decost, *RED INDIAN EXPERIENCES*, London: George Allen and Unwin, 1949. South Dakota Writers' Project, *LEGENDS OF THE MIGHTY SIOUX*, Vermillion: University of South Dakota, 1941. Standing Bear, Luther, *STORIES OF THE SIOUX*, Boston: Houghton Mifflin, 1934. Stands in Timber and Margot Liberty, *CHEYENNE MEMORIES*, New Haven: Yale University Press, 1967. Wissler, Clark, and D.C. Duvall, *MYTHOLOGY OF THE BLACKFOOT INDIANS*, Anthropological Papers of the Museum of Natural History, Vol. 2, Pt., 1, New York, 1908.